For little Jasmine

ORCHARD BOOKS

338 Euston Road, London NW1 3BH

Orchard Books Australia

Level 17/207 Kent Street, Sydney, NSW 2000

First published in 2009 by Orchard Books

ISBN 978 1 84616 321 0

A CIP catalogue record for this book
is available from the British Library.

10 9 8 7 6 5 4 3 2 1

Printed in China

Orchard Books is a division of
Hachette Children's Books,
an Hachette UK company.
www.hachette.co.uk

One More Hug for Nutmeg

Caroline Jayne Church

ORCHARD BOOKS

"Time for bed, Nutmeg,"

called Mummy.

So Nutmeg put away
her toys,

washed her
whiskers,

brushed her
teeth

and pulled on
her pyjamas.

As the little mouse snuggled
under the covers, Mummy read
Nutmeg her favourite
bedtime story . . .

until Nutmeg looked
very sleepy.

"Night, night, Nutmeg," Mummy whispered,
giving her a bedtime kiss and a hug.

"Night, night, Mum," said Nutmeg,
as Mummy took out the lantern.

Nutmeg tried to sleep, but without
the lantern her room felt dark
and she felt lonely.

"MUM," she called.

"Just one more thing . . .
Please may I have Molly Mouse
to keep me company?"

So Mummy fetched Molly Mouse
and gave Nutmeg **one more hug**
good night.

But Nutmeg still
couldn't sleep.
Now she was thirsty.

"MUM!" she called.
"Just one more
thing . . ."

So Mummy gave
Nutmeg a cup
of warm milk

and a cosy blanket and
one more hug
good night.

The extra blanket and drink made Nutmeg
feel lovely and warm, but then she heard
a strange noise!
"MUM!" she called.
"Just one more thing . . .
I need my woolly hat to cover
my ears."

So Mummy brought Nutmeg's hat and gently
tucked it round her ears,
and gave her **one more hug . . .**

blew   her

and

one

more

kiss . . .

as she closed the door.

Nutmeg now had Molly Mouse, a drink,
another blanket and a woolly hat . . .
but still she could not sleep!

What was missing? wondered Nutmeg.

And then she realised.

"MUM!" called Nutmeg.

"Just one more thing . . .

All I need now to get me off

to sleep is . . . .

ONE MORE

HUG!"

So Mummy gave her little Nutmeg one last . . .

GREAT BIG HUG.

"And just one last thing,
I promise,"
whispered Nutmeg . . .

But Mummy
was already fast asleep.